The Blue Glass Heart

For my brother, David Zeldis, whose long-ago
collection of sea glass still shimmers in my memory
–Y.Z.M.

To my Alberto. My love.
–C.F.

KAR-BEN PUBLISHING®
An imprint of Lerner Publishing Group, Inc.
241 First Avenue North
Minneapolis, MN 55401 USA

Website address: www.karben.com

Main body text set in ITC Avand Garde Gothic Std.
Typeface provided by International Typeface Corp.

Library of Congress Cataloging-in-Publication Data TK

Names: McDonough, Yona Zeldis, author. | Fedele, Chiara, illustrator.
Title: The blue glass heart / Yona Zeldis McDonough ; illustrated by Chiara Fedele.
Description: Minneapolis : Kar-Ben Publishing, (2023) | Audience: Ages 3–8. | Audience:
    Grades 2–3. | Summary: When eight-year-old Sarah accidentally breaks Bubbe's blue glass
    bowl, she sets a heart-shaped piece of blue glass on an adventure, touching the lives of
    children around the world, until it remarkably finds its way back home.
Identifiers: LCCN 2022015392 (print) | LCCN 2022015393 (ebook) | ISBN 9781728445526 (library
    binding) | ISBN 9781728445533 (paperback) | ISBN 9781728481081 (ebook)
Subjects: CYAC: Lost and found possessions—Fiction. | LCGFT: Picture books.
Classification: LCC PZ7.M15655 Bl 2023 (print) | LCC PZ7.M15655 (ebook) | DDC (E)—dc23

LC record available at https://lccn.loc.gov/2022015392
LC ebook record available at https://lccn.loc.gov/2022015393

Manufactured in the United States of America
1-50249-49866-7/6/2022

The Blue Glass Heart

Yona Zeldis McDonough

illustrated by Chiara Fedele

KAR-BEN
PUBLISHING

The blue glass bowl sits on the countertop.
It is filled with lemons.

Sarah's not supposed to touch the bowl. But the way the light streams through the color is so beautiful. She has to touch it. Just once.

CRASH!
Lemons roll everywhere, mixed with bright pieces of shattered glass.

Bubbe rushes over. "Are you hurt?"

Sarah's heart is pounding. "No. But I broke your bowl." Her eyes fill with tears.

"That's all right," Bubbe says. "I can replace the bowl. I can't replace you." She holds her granddaughter close before she sweeps up the glass.

Later, Sarah spies a piece of glass Bubbe missed. It has one smooth edge. The rest is sharp and tapers down to a point, so that it looks like a triangle. Sarah puts it in her pocket.

The next day, Sarah and Bubbe each pay a nickel to take the subway to Coney Island. Sarah runs to the water. She comes out only when her teeth start to chatter.

Sarah builds a sandcastle and puts the piece of blue glass on the top. Perfect!

When the tide rushes in, the moat fills with water. But the next wave knocks down the castle. The bit of blue glass is carried away, lost in the churning waves.

A gull swoops down, spying the piece of glass in the water.
But he decides it's not something to eat. The ocean settles,
and the piece of glass drifts calmly along.

Palm trees sway in the wind. The bit of glass has washed ashore in Florida. Benny is collecting shells in his tin pail. He picks up the pretty piece of glass and puts it in his pail to show his mother.

He doesn't know the pail has a hole. The piece of glass slips out and is swept away. Bobbing on the turquoise water, the glass sparkles when the sun hits it.

The bit of glass floats all the way to a beach in Venezuela, where Dulcinea and her father are gathering clams. Dulcinea does not notice the piece of glass, as it floats into her basket.

Dulcinea's mother does not see the glass either, and it ends up in the fish stew. "Look what I found," Dulcinea says.

"It's a good thing you didn't bite it!" says her mother. "That must mean the glass is lucky."

Dulcinea puts the piece of glass in her pocket.

She is still asleep the next morning when her mother takes the clothes down to wash. The piece of blue glass slips out of the pocket and into the water. Off it travels to the sea once more.

The glass floats past starfish and jellyfish.

It brushes past a whale.

It flutters through a school of sharks.

A lobster picks up the piece of blue glass but then drops it back into the sea.

A storm carries the piece of glass to Tel Aviv, where Dov finds it on the beach. The blue glass looks magical to him.

Dov tells his daughter Yael that the family is leaving Tel Aviv and moving to New York for his new job. He gives her the piece of glass to remind her of Israel.

This time, the piece of glass travels not in the water but in a sleek, silver plane that pierces the sky.

Yael doesn't like New York. It's cold. No one speaks Hebrew. The other kids tease her. All except Ruth. Ruth teaches her English words, and Yael teaches her Hebrew words. Ruth invites Yael to the playground and then to play at her apartment.

Yael wants to give Ruth, her first friend in the new city, a present. But what? Suddenly she knows: the piece of blue glass. She puts it in a box and ties a ribbon around it. She gives the box to Ruth.

Ruth's mouth forms a little *O* of delight when she opens the box.

"It's so pretty! It looks like a blue glass heart."

Ruth hugs Yael. They will be Best Friends Forever.

Ruth shows the blue glass heart to her mother.

"Your great-grandma Sarah loved that color," her mother says. "When she was little, her bubbe had a blue glass bowl that your great-grandma broke. When she grew up, she collected blue glass bowls that reminded her of the broken one."

"Maybe this is a piece of Great-Grandma Sarah's bowl," Ruth says.

"That's not too likely," laughs her mother. "But it's lovely just the same."

Ruth places the blue glass heart on the windowsill.
When the sun is at just the right angle, light comes
streaming through. The blue glass heart shines
steadily, just like a precious jewel.